AMANDA AND THE MAGIC GARDEN

AMANDA
AND THE
MAGIC GARDEN

By John Himmelman

Viking Kestrel

VIKING KESTREL
Viking Penguin Inc., 40 West 23rd Street, New York, New York 10010, U.S.A.
Penguin Books Ltd, Harmondsworth, Middlesex, England
Penguin Books Australia Ltd, Ringwood, Victoria, Australia
Penguin Books Canada Limited, 2801 John Street, Markham, Ontario, Canada L3R 1B4
Penguin Books (N.Z.) Ltd, 182–190 Wairau Road, Auckland 10, New Zealand

First published in 1987 by Viking Penguin Inc.
Published simultaneously in Canada

Library of Congress Cataloging in Publication Data
Himmelman, John.   Amanda and her magic garden.
Summary: Amanda's garden, grown from magic seeds,
is a great success until its vegetables cause the
animals who eat them to grow to giant size.
[1. Gardens—Fiction. 2. Size—Fiction.
3. Animals—Fiction. 4. Magic—Fiction] I. Title.
PZ7.H5686A1   1987   [E]   86-15841   ISBN 0-670-80823-7

Printed in Japan by Dai Nippon Printing Co. Ltd.
Set in Bookman Light
1   2   3   4   5   90   89   88   87

*This story is dedicated to Dad
and to Blue-1 Footed Boobies, Talking Mongeese,
and the many other stories he read to his sons.*

One quiet morning, while Amanda the
witch was busy with her chores,
Greenmoss the troll stopped by for a visit.

"Would you like to buy some magic?" he asked.

"I have all the magic I need," she said politely.

"Well, have you anything to eat? I usually stop for a snack about now."

Amanda invited him in. The troll
showed her his wares while they munched
on marshmallows.

"Are you sure you don't need a magic stick? It turns butterflies into moths."
"No, that would be mean," said Amanda.

"Well, how about this magic rock? It grows warts on anything."
"That's not very nice," said Amanda.

"This magic sneezing dust can be fun."

"Achoo," said Amanda. "Don't you sell anything that doesn't cause trouble?"

"Well, I do have these giant vegetable seeds. Take them as a gift. Feed the whole forest."

"Thank you, I think," said Amanda.

When the troll went on his way, Amanda
examined the seeds. "They look harmless
enough," she thought. She set right to
work planting her garden.

The weeks passed and her garden grew
and grew.

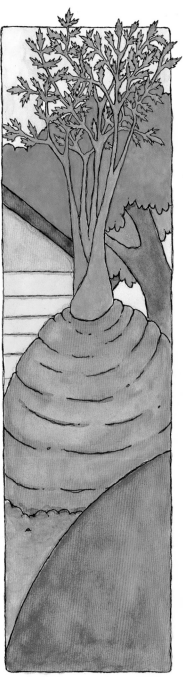

Amanda loved spending time in her
giant garden. It was certainly one of a kind.

The day finally came to pick her first
tomato. Amanda started to wheel it in,
but she didn't look where she was going.

The witch landed right on top of Art the rabbit.

"How do you do?" he asked.

"I'm doing all right," she answered, "but you seem a bit large this morning."

"I wonder how he got so big?" thought Amanda.
"Could he have been eating my vegetables?"

That would explain why there was a
twenty-foot squirrel stuck in her chimney.
"Shrink!" she whispered, aiming her
wand at the squirrel. Nothing happened.

"I'll have to try a different approach. *Grow!*" she shouted to the chimney. The chimney grew, and the squirrel shot down and squeezed out the front door.

As the days passed, more and more giant animals kept popping up. "There's got to be a solution," she thought. She tried to sleep but the sounds of colossal crickets kept her awake.

The next morning, as Amanda was trying different spells on the garden, she noticed a huge skunk sleeping under a tree. "Don't anyone startle him," she whispered.

The skunk began to stir.

"Quickly, everybody sing a lullaby!" said
Amanda. All the animals joined in until
the skunk fell back asleep.

Just as they finished the song, Amanda spotted a hungry-looking bear holding a piece of turnip. "No, wait!" she cried.

The bear panicked and ran toward Amanda's house.

Amanda raced in after him. "Don't eat
that turnip!" she warned.

"Oh, don't be selfish," said the bear, and
he popped the turnip into his mouth.

Soon the bear took up the entire room.

"I guess I shouldn't have eaten it," he
said.

"Well, you didn't know better," said the
witch consolingly.

"All this from a tiny turnip," she moaned.

Suddenly, Amanda got an idea.

She ran behind her house and went right to work. In a few short hours she had grown a miniature vegetable garden.

"If the troll's giant vegetables made the animals grow, then my small ones should make them shrink," she reasoned.

Amanda's idea was a success. Soon all
the animals shrank to their proper size.

Later that evening, Amanda cut down what was left of the giant vegetables. She noticed that one tiny carrot still remained from her miniature garden.

She plucked it up and took it inside. It might make a nice snack for a certain mischievous troll.